# The Bear Hunt

*by Christoffer Petersen*

# THE BEAR HUNT

Published by Aarluuk Press

ISBN: 978-87-93680-20-3

www.christoffer-petersen.com

## Author's Note

*The Bear Hunt* was originally titled *Arnannguaq's Prize*, and I confess to writing it quite a while ago. I wrote it in a fabulous school hall that doubled as a library for the school and the local community in the settlement of Kullorsuaq, an island in the Upernavik area of North West Greenland. The Danish name for the island is *Djævelens Tommelfinger*, which means *The Devil's Thumb*. The island has a striking mountain that looks quite thumb-like from the air. I saw it as I flew in on a helicopter for my role as external examiner for the English exams in Kullorsuaq. It was early June, and the island was still locked in ice. I remember sleeping in the school pantry. I felt like Harry Potter.

The original idea for *The Bear Hunt* came from a picture in Ivars Silis' book *My White World: Thirty Years with a Camera in Greenland* (2000). It is an incredible book, full of rich photographs of an amazing people and their country. I was hooked on the photos of a polar bear hunt, and how the dogs pulling the sledge were released to hunt as bear dogs. While I would prefer, personally, that polar bears were not hunted, the image was captivating, and it sparked a story.

# THE BEAR HUNT

This is that story.

So, if you're curious, you might want to join Âjak and Tulugaq on the first of what I hope will be many Greenland adventures – not crime, as such, but crimes of one kind or another will inevitably play a role in several of the stories. Each short story will take about twenty-five minutes to read, but I hope the imagery stays with you much longer, just like Ivars Silis' photographs, and my own memories of Greenland.

Chris
*January 2019*
*Denmark*

CHRISTOFFER PETERSEN

# The Bear Hunt

# 1

Fourteen dogs clawed at the smooth, hard ice as they sped forward, the gang lines bouncing as they pulled the long, broad sledge smartly across the ice. The dogs could smell *nanoq*, the ice bear, its scent intoxicating, elusive but close. Suddenly veering west, the lead dog located the musky, damp smell of *nanoq* at the edge of the ice. The two men gripping the sledge could also see him now, a large male, lifting his nose and scenting danger.

"You must cut the lines now, brother," Tulugaq shouted over the grating ice.

"Not yet, we're too far away," Âjak said. "The dogs will be alone."

"But they won't catch him if they must pull us, too. Cut the lines, brother."

Âjak flashed a hard stare at his older brother and pointedly cracked the whip on the ice. At the sound of the whip, the dogs picked up speed as the ice bear finally recognised the threat and began to lope away.

"Now Âjak, release the dogs," Tulugaq said, gripping his brother's shoulder.

Âjak shook him off and then, grudgingly, drew the sledge-knife from its seal-skin scabbard lashed tightly to the sledge. With a last glance at the bear, he leaned forward, gripping a sledge runner with one hand, sawing through the taut lines with the knife in the other. As each dog was released from the burden of the sledge, it flew across the ice. Nivi, the lead dog, was the last to be cut free, and she raced to regain her position at the front of the pack. The sledge slid sideways to a grinding halt as the two men grabbed their spears and knives and ran after the dogs.

*Nanoq* turned its great head at the sound of the fifty-some feet clawing their way across the ice. The ice bear began to run as they closed the gap, choosing not to swim before it had to. But as the first dog sank his teeth into its rear left paw, it turned and batted the dog into the sea. More dogs attacked, snarling and yelping and then silent as their teeth took hold of the bear's yellow fur. Two more dogs were launched into the sea as the bear struck with alternating front paws, its claws raking the belly of one dog, while teeth flew from the jaws of two more. But they were wearing him down. The bear roared as it struck, backing towards the edge of the ice.

Nivi was there to stop it.

She snarled once before springing at the bear's throat, her jaws clamping shut as her teeth punctured the thick ruff of fur around the bear's neck. The bear faltered, tiring from the sustained attacks on all sides. It was then that the men arrived.

Tulugaq took hold of several of the dogs' lines, winding them around his fist, striking hard at the noses of the dogs that turned on him in their blood lust. Âjak faced the ice bear and plunged his broad-bladed spear into the bear's side, thrusting sharply upwards, careful not to nick his lead dog locked at the bear's throat. Tulugaq cast his spear along the ice to his brother as he gripped more lines and pulled still more dogs away from the dying bear. Âjak took the spear and slowly approached this once proud prince of Arctic beasts, standing before him as the ice bear glowered weakly into his eyes.

"*Tassa*, Nivi," Âjak said.

The lead dog released her grip, retreating as she did so. Renewed, the bear began to rise just as Âjak plunged the second spear into its heart.

Before the bear could exhale its dying breath, Âjak drew his knife and began cutting through the skin to carve meat for the dogs, the immediate reward after a successful kill. Nivi received the first piece, and she ate it there in the shadow of the great ice bear as the sun picked its way through the ragged clouds above. The other dogs fought for the warm, bloody meat as Âjak threw chunks onto the ice and Tulugaq released them one at a time. Two of the three dogs launched into the sea had perished and a third clung to the ice edge. Tulugaq heaved it up. Âjak threw another chunk of meat to the shivering dog as it shook off the water of the Arctic Sea.

Âjak withdrew the spears and cleaned them quickly on the bear's fur. He returned to the mouth of the great beast and sliced off its tongue.

"Here, Nivi. What a fine dog you are," Âjak said, as he kneeled down to feed his lead dog the prize piece of the kill.

Tulugaq joined him as the dogs licked the blood off the ice. Some had already begun to lie down and pant, their long tongues steamed in the chill night air at the edge of the ice.

"A good kill brother."

"I lost two dogs," Âjak said, one hand fondling Nivi's ears.

"*Aap*, but a good kill nonetheless; a small price for Arnannguaq's prize. Let's make camp here and move on tomorrow."

Âjak nodded and walked back to the sledge.

## 2

"We will be in Nuugaatsiaq in two days if the weather holds," Tulugaq said, between mouthfuls of succulent bear meat. "Arnannguaq will be there."

Âjak said nothing. He chewed his meat, picking fat from the bone with his fingers and sucking them noisily.

"Of course, brother, she might choose another man with more conversation." The crow's feet around Tulugaq's eyes creased as he smiled.

Âjak stopped chewing.

"What do you know, brother?" he said, rising to a sitting position.

Tulugaq stopped smiling. He had seen this jealous side of Âjak far too often.

"Nothing, Âjak. Really, nothing. I'm teasing. Enjoy your meat before it becomes cold." Tulugaq lay down on the reindeer skins covering the floor of their tent.

"You know something." Âjak pointed the bone at his older brother accusingly. "You are a shaman. Tell me what you know."

Tulugaq sighed and glanced around the tent before looking his brother dead in the eyes.

"There is nothing to tell. I would rather praise your dogs and enjoy this warm meat."

"Speak shaman," Âjak said. "I demand it. The

hot food in your belly is payment enough for your future-sight. Tell me or you will sleep with the dogs."

"I owe you nothing, brother. This kill is ours. Did you achieve this all by yourself?" Tulugaq sat upright, tense within the confines of the tent. "You needed me today. I held back your dogs and fished another right out of Sedna's death-grip. Don't threaten me."

The two men stared at each other. The icy wind outside the tent struggled to match the atmosphere within. Finally, a dog howled; it was Nivi raising her voice to the wind. The pack of bear-dogs quickly joined her. The brothers relaxed slightly and looked about the tent.

"I need to know, brother," Âjak breathed. "I am in doubt."

"If you ask me as a shaman, I am bound to tell you the truth," Tulugaq said.

"I ask you as shaman, as is my right as a hunter with a fresh kill on his sledge."

"Very well, *hunter*. Make me some tea."

Âjak put his bone to one side and wiped his greasy hands on his seal-skin smock. He positioned a pot of ice, fished from the sea, above the blubber lamp and waited for it to melt. Tulugaq glanced once at his brother and began to remove his clothing. He sat but a few moments later upon the reindeer skin wearing nothing but an amulet of polished whalebone about his neck. This he held in his right hand. With his left hand he clasped the hand of the hunter.

The bubbling of the water soothed the shaman's

mind as the steam from the pot warmed the tent. Tulugaq could feel the sweat bead on his bare skin, dripping from his brow onto his nose and stinging his eyes. It was time to push, to force the heat from his own body and thus break his way into the spirit world. He contracted his muscles and held them so, willing the heat from his own body, bringing about a chill from his very bones to the surface of his skin. Âjak watched, captivated, as beads of sweat became gelatinous, then crystalline, then fully rounded tiny balls of ice that trilled down the shaman's arms, and tumbled from his brow. The ice beads in his hair remained trapped for the time being, while his eyelashes merged in a web of rime, giving the impression of opaque, empty eye sockets, blind to this world, staring into another.

Âjak felt alone in the tent, his body confused by the bubbling heat, and the sight of the iceman that was his brother before him. The passage of time when the shaman roamed the spirit realm was immeasurable. Âjak knew this and sat silently, waiting, the icy hand of the shaman slowly cold-burning his own.

Tulugaq blinked through ice-encrusted eyes. He could see the settlement of Nuugaatsiaq in the distance. Chilled and wary, he took long silent strides towards the village. He could see Arnannguaq's dwelling and he moved his mind closer, willing himself into the warm light of the room, the shine of which pierced the film of ice covering his eyes giving him an insect-like view, the details projected and repeated sharply about his field of vision. Arnannguaq was crying, now laughing, then deadly serious in her lovemaking with another man. He was of normal height; he wore the clothes of a hunter and yet his face was hidden by the hair of the woman astride him. Every time Tulugaq tried to see the man's face from another angle, Arnannguaq moved and thwarted him. It was useless, but it was clear that this man was not the hunter; Âjak was nowhere to be seen. Although Tulugaq did not recognise him, the man seemed common enough; perhaps one of the hunters from the settlement? His manner and dress were indeed local, and he was clearly known to Arnannguaq.

Tiring, Tulugaq resisted the pull of his own warm tent a moment more and constructed a hasty spirit-fence around Arnannguaq's turf hut. He appealed to Âmo, the shaman's familiar with long, protective arms. Tulugaq hoped it would be enough to restrain anyone wishing harm to those inside.

Having seen enough, Tulugaq relaxed his muscles, let the warmth of the tent thaw his skin, the bubbling water ease his mind and the smell of seal blubber ferry his senses fully into the living world. The tent shifted into focus as the ice beads in his hair streamed in thin rivulets down his body, pooling among the stiff fibres of the reindeer skins covering the ice floor.

Tulugaq released the hunter's hand and asked for tea. Âjak knew not to hurry the shaman and set about pouring the boiling water into a cup, adding dried herbs as he did so. The shaman pulled on his clothes and wiped the cold sweat and the dark vision from his eyes, breathing a silent plea to Âmo as he did so.

Âjak handed the shaman his tea and waited.

After some time, he could wait no longer. He looked at the shaman, his hands gripping the reindeer skin beneath him.

"Tell me, shaman," he whispered.

Tulugaq looked at his brother. Then the shaman spoke to the hunter.

"There is another," he said.

## 3

Âjak packed in a rage, frantically tying the tent to the sledge. He almost dragged the carcass of the bear onto the ice, but Tulugaq prevented him. Âjak ripped the dogs' lines from the ice-anchors and dragged them to the sledge. They seemed to understand their master's mood and were quickly cowed into formation. All save Nivi. Curious about the sudden activity, Nivi tried several times to lick Âjak's hand, only to be rewarded with a smart cuff about the ears. Further attempts at contact were rewarded by a sharp kick to the stomach as Nivi was finally placed at the head of the pack.

Tulugaq had expected a sudden departure, but even he was surprised at the ferocity of his brother's actions. He stood ready to spring onto the sledge as Âjak cracked the whip about the dogs and bullied them into motion. Tulugaq barely caught the sledge as it leaped into the air. Âjak landed heavily as he sprang onto the front of the sledge, narrowly missing the front runners. They sat in grave silence astride the dead ice bear as the dogs raced ahead of their master's fury.

After a short time, the dogs began to falter as the added weight of the ice bear slowed them down. Âjak began to crack the whip mercilessly, and the speed increased again.

"Easy brother," Tulugaq said, resting a hand upon Âjak's shoulder.

Âjak shrugged him off and continued to crack the whip on the ice, the sharp retort echoing about the approaching mountains of the Nuussuaq peninsula. As they drew further and further away from the open sea, the ice began to change, affected by the tides along the coastline. Huge daggers of ice appeared before them, and even Âjak had to concede that they must slow down in order to get past these natural barriers.

The two men worked together to manhandle the sledge, Âjak in front leading the dogs with Tulugaq pushing from behind. Nivi tried her best to keep up with her master, but, weary from her struggle with the ice bear, she began to tire. The dogs became anxious as she slipped further behind. Several times, her lines became so entangled with the ice that Âjak had to stop and free her. He cursed her every time he did so, and, once free, Nivi crept away from his wrath.

As the way ahead suddenly became smooth, Âjak leapt onto the sledge as the dogs picked up speed. Tulugaq, holding onto the wooden uprights at the rear, kicked his way rapidly onto the sledge. Nivi was caught out by the sudden increase in pace. She missed her footing and became caught in her own lines. Unable to get to her feet, she was swept under a sledge runner, its combined weight of man and bear crushing her ribs. She passed beneath the sledge and was pulled along, breathless, bruised and bloody. Âjak looked at her once before drawing his knife and cutting her line free. The sledge gained speed as Nivi lay helpless in its wake.

"Stop now, Âjak. This is too much." Tulugaq said. He glanced at Nivi on the ice; the dog's body shrank as the distance increased.

Âjak stared at his brother.

"We're too heavy for just eleven dogs. Stop now. Please."

Âjak said nothing. He stared at his brother and at the knife still in his hand. Tulugaq followed his gaze down to the sledge knife and then looked sharply up at his brother's face. Âjak's face was stern and hate glazed his eyes. Tulugaq moved back along the sledge until he could retreat no further. Âjak looked at him and slowly sheathed the knife. As Tulugaq relaxed, Âjak beckoned him forward.

"You are right, brother, we are too heavy," Âjak said, forcing a smile.

Tulugaq smiled back. Pleased at this change in his brother's mood.

They faced each other, each sitting with legs astride the carcass of the ice bear they had worked hard to kill. The breath of the dogs evaporated in the icy air as they ran. The ice ground noisily beneath the runners where, but a moment ago, Nivi, Âjak's most prized bear-dog, had been horribly crushed.

"We're too heavy," Tulugaq said. "Will you stop?"

"No, shaman," Âjak said. "We will not stop."

Tulugaq looked at him, confusion clouding his sense.

"But the sledge *is* too heavy."

As Tulugaq stared at his brother, Âjak leaped at

him, pushing the shaman off balance. Tulugaq fell from the sledge, grasping the bottom of a wooden upright as his body was dragged like an anchor across the ice. The dogs slowed, some turning in their uncertainty. Feeling the sudden drop in speed, Âjak stood on the sledge and looked down at the man that was his brother. He took a last look at him before kicking Tulugaq's hand free of the sledge.

"Goodbye, *shaman,*" he shouted as the dogs returned to a more pleasing pace.

Tulugaq lay on the ice watching the sledge grow smaller in the distance.

## 4

The sledge slowed as Âjak approached Nuugaatsiaq, almost as if the dogs sensed the coming tragedy that their master was about to deliver.

Âjak too was quiet, his thoughts narrowing as he became anxious as to the truth of the shaman's words. He imagined entering Arnannguaq's dwelling and finding her there with the other man. He did not doubt he would be quickly rid of his competitor. Arnannguaq would accept her prize, and he would be both a successful hunter and her chosen mate. Âjak's status within the village would rise, and no one would question his right to have killed the man who would steal Arnannguaq away from him.

The sledge stopped in its tracks, as did Âjak's thoughts. The dogs were dead tired and without the continuous prompting from their master, they had naturally drawn to a halt. Âjak would have to walk from here. Arriving quietly on foot would also give him the advantage. He would surprise his adversary. He untied the sealskin cords, lashing the spear to the sledge and tugged it free.

Arnannguaq's turf hut was at the far end of the settlement. He could see the faint glow of the seal-blubber lamps spilling softly out of the cracks within the walls. The snow muffled Âjak's approach, but strangely, with every step, the spear grew heavier in his hands until he was forced to abandon it. Each subsequent step pulled at the knife sheathed on the belt at his waist. He drew it and cast it aside. His hands, his only remaining weapons, hung heavy at his sides. The faint pressure of a spirit's grip around each ankle gave him pause. He wondered at the power of the shaman. As he reached the door to the hut he needed all his energy to push it inwards.

Arnannguaq looked up as Âjak moved into the light. Her smile of surprise quickly faded as she saw the grim look on his face. The young man at her side looked up sharply at the sound of a terrible wailing coming from the intruder. He did not recognise the face of his sister's lover.

Âjak took hold of the young man by the throat, his fingers squeezing the last breath out of his would-be competitor. Her brother struggled, surprise and confusion aiding his attacker, while Arnannguaq, roused into desperate action, clawed at Âjak's face, tearing the flesh down his cheeks. Blood dripped and pooled under his chin, where it stayed briefly before flowing onto his chest. Arnannguaq's brother could neither breathe nor scream as Âjak strangled the last remaining life from his body. He hung suddenly, heavy and limp in the hunter's hands as his eyes glazed over.

Arnannguaq watched her brother die and heard her own screams evaporate in the cold gust of air as the door of the hut burst inwards. Two men wrestled Âjak away from the younger man and threw him into the snow outside. Âjak pushed himself to his feet and faced the men briefly before turning and running through the village towards the mountain, Arnannguaq's sobbing ringing in his ears.

A short distance up the mountainside, Âjak turned to see activity in the settlement. Beams of light pierced the darkness intermittently as door after door was opened and shut, as hunters and wives, children and dogs trampled tragic lines of sorrow in the snow between the huts.

Âjak, the great hunter, was now nothing more than a common *qivittoq*, an outcast, abandoning his people and his home out of a jealous and meaningless rage. He had killed his lover's brother, a young man, a lowly hunter with but a few kills to his name, hardly a competitor for the love of his own sister. The shaman had been wrong. He had killed needlessly and effectively ended his own life. For what?

Âjak vowed there and then that he would seek out his shaman brother and put an end to his false prophecies. He would gouge out his eyes and feed them to the ravens that gave the shaman his name. Vengeance would be Âjak's last act as a human before he adopted completely the life of the *qivittoq*.

As he watched the flow of grieving family and friends continue between the huts, he saw the body of the young man brought out of Arnannguaq's hut. It was wrapped gently in skins and carried to the burial place at the rear of the village. Four men placed the body in a shallow pit in the ground, one of several dug the previous summer. They stood to one side while Arnannguaq, her mother and father, and two small sisters began to place large stones around his body. Once encircled with stones, they too stood to one side and watched as people from the settlement added more. The four men who had carried him finally covered the young man's body with several large slabs, protecting him from scavenging animals and shielding him from the eyes of his murderer, hiding above them on the mountainside.

Âjak saw all this and watched too as his dogs were taken from their traces and the ice bear removed from the sledge. Hunters and their wives began to flense the meat from the bones. The Arctic in winter was not a place to refuse meat, no matter who had provided it.

## 5

Tulugaq approached the village cautiously. He was tired, but otherwise unhurt. During the past two days alone on the ice, he had imagined the scene that would meet him in Nuugaatsiaq many times. There was no sign of Âjak's sledge or dogs, though there was a lot of blood on the snow where he guessed the ice bear had been butchered. Tulugaq walked on into the village.

A hunter repairing his kayak in anticipation of the coming thaw saw the shaman and hailed him. They talked quickly and quietly together, and Tulugaq soon knew the fate that had befallen the young man, though he struggled to believe that Arnannguaq's brother had also been her lover. As a shaman, Tulugaq had learned long ago that his future-sight was often accurate but subject to interpretation. He had long since stopped second guessing himself, but he had always told his visions in their entirety for the very reason that there were many ways to interpret them. In the case of Âjak however, he should perhaps have lied. The fact that he had not had caused the death of the young man now buried beneath an ice bear's weight in stone.

Tulugaq walked deliberately to Arnannguaq's turf hut and found the door ajar. Peering in, he saw Arnannguaq and her family sitting on reindeer skins around a lamp, burning still in the daylight in memory of her brother. He entered and sat at the feet of her father.

The family acknowledged his presence, and he listened to their grief-stricken tale. They asked him for comfort and when he found none he could offer, he suggested instead that he prepare a soothing tea to help them sleep. None of them had done so since that murderous night.

Tulugaq sang softly as they drank the tea and slowly crawled into the sleeping space beside one another. All except Arnannguaq, who took great comfort in the shaman's voice and leaned against his side. As the family slept, Arnannguaq made herself comfortable in the shaman's arms.

After some time, Arnannguaq moved slightly and looked up into the face of Tulugaq. The weather-lines upon his face accentuated in the lamplight appealed to her and she turned to face him. Wearied by his journey, Tulugaq was slow to perceive the change in Arnannguaq. Only when she sat astride his legs, did he realise that she was in need of something more than a shaman's soothing powers. She kissed him fully upon his lips. He kissed back, her long, jet-black hair tickling his face. They kissed for a long time. Arnannguaq's hair tickled him often, but every time Tulugaq tried to free himself of her hair, to kiss her neck, Arnannguaq moved and his face remained hidden from view.

They made love, gently at first and then more passionately, as Arnannguaq forced her grief out of her body and into the shaman's. He could grieve for them both, for the loss of her brother and for the betrayal of his own.

As the short winter day turned into the long winter night, Arnannguaq crawled into the sleeping space and shared her warmth with her two small sisters, shivering slightly from the creeping cold accompanying the enveloping darkness. Tulugaq rose slowly and walked out of the hut into the polar night.

A pale white arc of Northern Lights bridged the black sky between the mountains. Despite such sorrow, it would be a fair day tomorrow. Tulugaq, tracing the northern lights with his eyes, worried that Âmo had perhaps abandoned him? His thoughts turned to Âjak and with such thoughts, there settled a storm-cloud about the shaman's heart. The long winter night was but one of many – ample time for his brother to exact his revenge. Tulugaq wondered if he would live to see the summer.

*The End*

## About the Author

Christoffer Petersen is the author's pen name. He lives in Denmark. Chris started writing stories about Greenland while teaching in Qaanaaq, the largest village in the very north of Greenland – the population peaked at 600 during the two years he lived there. Chris spent a total of seven years in Greenland, teaching in remote communities and at the Police Academy in the capital of Nuuk.

You can find Chris in Denmark or online here:
www.christoffer-petersen.com

For exclusive content check out
Christoffer Petersen's Patreon page
www.patreon.com/christofferpetersen

CHRISTOFFER PETERSEN

Similar novels and stories from the same author

*The Ice Circus*
*Northwind*
*Yule at Aurora Station*
*Twelvetyde*
*Witch Bluff*
*Witch Hunt*
*Witch Born*